PRAISE FOR

Football Magic

"Throughout my career in sports, I've had many magical
moments. Reading *Football Magic: Buddy's New Beginning* reminded
me of the days I spent playing youth football, learning the
importance of teamwork and the true magic of football."

— Doug Flutie, 1984 Heisman Trophy Winner
and former NFL quarterback

"Sean Stellato scores a touchdown with this
tale of teamwork, courage, and determination—
traits any superstar athlete should have!"

— Adam Schefter, ESPN, NFL Insider

"Everybody has a mountain to climb and Stellato shows us
how to do it with high spirits and a positive attitude. Sports
help us on our journey, and Stellato navigates with style."

— Beth Mowins, play-by-play sports announcer
and journalist, ESPN and CBS

"The Football Magic series is a truly magical
read for parents and kids alike."

— John Harbaugh, head coach of the Baltimore Ravens

"We could all learn a thing or two from Buddy and
his friends. Through teamwork, grit, and a little
determination, there's no stopping the Witches!"

— Jon Gruden, head coach of the Oakland Raiders, former coach
of the 2002 Super Bowl champion Tampa Bay Buccaneers

"Buddy and his group of friends really show what it
means to be a team! They're every coach's dream!"

— Sean Payton, head coach of the New Orleans Saints

"Drawing from his love of sports, Stellato infuses the magic of
Salem into Buddy's thrilling story with a perfect pirouette."

— Boston Ballet

"*Buddy's New Beginning* perfectly captures the nerves,
pressure, and excitement that come along with being
the new kid in town and on the football field."

— Vinny Testaverde, Heisman Trophy winner
and first pick overall in the 1987 draft

"This children's book by Sean Stellato is an inspiration for all kids just like Buddy. I encourage anyone in the sports world and beyond to support literacy for our youth. *Football Magic: Buddy's New Beginning* ties both worlds together. I myself use my Read with Reed 83 program to help underserved kids in the Boys and Girls Club to catch the love of reading and tackle a good book. I'll definitely be using Stellato's book in my reading program nationwide."

— Andre Reed, 2014 NFL Hall of Fame wide receiver

"This engaging read subtly and magically convenes a lesson indispensable to every student, athlete, and person regardless of their age. Rising to the challenge, whether it be the first day in a new school or the Super Bowl, means focusing on the task of the moment rather than giving in to fear and pessimistic thinking. Stellato emphasizes both in this great read."

— Wayne L. Klein, PhD, clinical neuropsychologist, Spaulding Rehabilitation Hospital

"Stellato scores big with this amazing story. It reminds us of the true magic of sports and the opportunities to overcome adversity."

— Julie Foudy, two-time Olympic Gold Medalist and World Cup Champion

"This is a great story of learning what it takes to be a team of champions."

— Mike Eruzione, captain of the 1980 Miracle on Ice hockey team

Football Magic

www.mascotbooks.com

Football Magic: Buddy's New Beginning

Second printing. This Mascot Books edition published in 2021.

Illustrations by Chiara Savarese

For more information, please contact:
Mascot Books
620 Herndon Parkway, Suite 320
Herndon, VA 20170
info@mascotbooks.com

sean@seanstellato.com
www.seanstellato.com
@seanstellato
Sean Stellato
seanstellatoses

Library of Congress Control Number: 2019904423

CPSIA Code: PRV0921B
ISBN: 978-1-64307-382-8

Printed in the United States

To my Gianna,
your strength, athleticism, and willingness to fight
inspires me every second of every day.

My daughters Sophia, Giulietta, and Siena
whom I love and cherish.

St. Anthony of Padua Roman Catholic School

AT ST. FRANCIS OF ASSISI ROMAN CATHOLIC CHURCH

The students of St. Anthony of Padua Roman Catholic School were so blessed to have had the opportunity to welcome Sean Stellato to our campus to celebrate his book *Football Magic: A Pirate's Tale*. The Football Magic series he has written with his daughter, Gianna, showcases the importance of determination, friendship, and believing in yourself. It was an incredible day for our students and staff to attend his presentation and receive his important message about keeping your faith at the center of all your actions. Sean literally brought Football Magic to life for the students and engaged with them effortlessly. I look forward to welcoming him back to our campus for another memorable visit.

Dr. Danielle Miller, Principal
St. Anthony of Padua Catholic School

SAINT FRANCIS
OF
A S S I S I

ROMAN CATHOLIC CHURCH
HENDERSON, NEVADA

I feel so blessed that Sean made the time to come to St. Anthony of Padua Roman Catholic School to talk to our students about his book *No Backing Down: The Inspirational Sto,y of the 1994 Salem High School Football Team*, the follow-up to his bestseller *Football Magic, Buddy's New Beginning*. Sean's marvelous presentation brought to life his message about persevering and working hard to achieve the goals we set ourselves. I know his talk inspired our students to appreciate their many blessings and to use the gifts and talents God has given them to overcome adversity, help others, and realize their dreams. Sean really connects with and motivates our young people, and I eagerly look forward to his next inspirational visit.

Fr. John Assalone, Pastor
St. Francis of Assisi Roman Catholic Church and St. Anthony of Padua Roman Catholic School

CHAPTER 1
Magical Beginnings

Buddy anxiously sat in the back seat of his grandma Owa's car. He had the window cracked, as he often got carsick. Loud bass-pumping hip-hop music blared from another car as they came to a stop at a traffic light. Buddy shook his head and thought of starting over: new school, new apartment, new friends, and a new team. Five new places in eleven years. This all made his stomach turn.

Buddy's dad had just been hired as the head football coach at Salem College.

Slowly they entered the city. A sign read "Salem, MA 1626." They passed the Hawthorne Hotel, which borders Salem Commons, and Salem Witch Museum was a stone's throw away.

At every corner Buddy saw shops, from card readers and Halloween costumes to the official witch store, which sent chills up his spine. That was one thing he was not sure he could get used to. Wicked Books caught his eye, as he loved to read, especially history books and mysteries. Grandma Owa slowly made her way onto Front Street, passing Old Burying Point Cemetery. The name Judge Hawthorne was listed at the entrance.

Grandma Owa slammed on the brakes as a black cat walked in front of the car. She immediately paused and touched her red bracelet. An old Italian wives tale, the color red is supposed to protect you from evil spirits. They turned down a narrow street where the Witchcraft Memorial sat. Stone benches honor the victims and preserve the legacy of those falsely accused.

Pulling onto Derby Street, Buddy rolled down the window and inhaled the fresh smell of the ocean. Kids ran up and down the Custom House steps playing tag. Pulling out an old map, they approached the House of Seven Gables.

Owa pulled up to a candy shop and handed him a crisp five-dollar bill. As he walked up to the door, he was amazed that the candy shop had been there since 1806. The smell of peppermint Gibraltars filled the air and made his eyes water. His eyes got wider as he observed all of the fudge. Buddy loved chocolate and fudge. He examined the ingredients because his sister had a peanut allergy. Picking out some items and a surprise for her, he exited the store.

They made their way up to Salem College to see where his dad worked, but his dad was not there. He walked by a statue and noticed it had the words his father always told him, "Dream, Believe, Achieve." He thought finally this may be a perfect long-term fit for his dad.

Towering trees lined the Salem Commons. Grandma Owa parked in front of a brick townhouse. A black and white "For Rent" sign was picketed into the ground. His dad always rented, as they moved often.

His dad had arrived weeks earlier, so he was excited to see him.

Buddy unfastened his seatbelt and saw that his eight-year-old sister Sophia was sound asleep. He tickled her ear to wake her up.

Owa pointed to the building next door, which was the Salem Witch Museum. "Looks like we will have a lot of constant neighbors," Owa said.

"I hope it's not haunted!" Sophia said as she got out of the car. Running as fast as she could, she yelled, "I get the room farthest away from the witches!"

"Sounds good to me," Buddy replied as they lugged their bags in.

As he walked into the apartment, Buddy noticed a small wooden plaque mounted to the building that read, "Built for Clifford Copperpot 'Merchant' 1914 Historic Salem." That caught Buddy's curiosity.

The empty apartment was bigger than their last one, and the smell of fresh paint was in the air. Time to make his room his own. Opening up boxes of his belongings, he pulled out his list of goals that would be hung in a special place. Taking out a folder from his backpack, he paused before opening it, smiling he examined the photo of his mom. It still was not easy after four years without her.

Buddy felt a familiar hand on his shoulder. "You have her eyes, son." He gave his dad a slight smile. Dad stood over him wearing a red sweatshirt that had *Salem College Football* across the chest. Holding back tears, Dad pulled him in for a big hug.

His dad told him to bring the rest of Grandma's boxes up.

"I will, and I will grab Sophia's things too." Buddy's head dropped as he slowly walked away.

"Buddy?" Dad's voice had a milder tone.

"Yeah, Dad?"

"Always remember to look up at the stars and not down at your feet. This is going to be our new home for a while." He tossed Buddy his keys. "Go into the basement and grab my brief-case out of my office."

Buddy hated basements, especially old and dark ones. The wooden steps cracked as he stepped on each one. A musty smell filled the air. Buddy could not stop thinking about how long he would be able to call this place home. A small ray of light glared through the window, and cobwebs covered almost every corner of the basement.

Halloween decorations were spread out on the floor. A witch's hat sat on top of a football that was enclosed in a glass case. He took the ball out of the case and examined it. The year 1914 was stitched along the seams in small lettering.

Seconds later, the electricity went off, causing him to stumble backwards and drop the ball. As the ball rolled away, it suddenly started to glow. He fell back and hit something hard.

The next thing he knew the lights were back on. He heard whimpering and could not make out what it was. At this point Buddy was spooked, but something in him itched to find the noise. He grabbed a broomstick for protection, making his way towards the sound.

He opened up a door, and it was love at first sight as a Boxer puppy sat in its cage. A note was taped to the door. Dad worked so much, which was hard on Buddy, and he often wrote Buddy notes.

Please read first before opening:

*Son, everyone needs a friend in a new
town. He loves to give tons of kisses.*

Love, Dad!

A strong sense of excitement entered Buddy's body. He scooped him up like a fumble and was instantly met with kisses. Carrying the football underneath his arm, he ran with joy as he bounded up the stairs, skipping every other step.

Owa had an excited look on her face. "Your dad is the king of surprises!"

Sophia grabbed the puppy, asking, "What's his name?"

"What's his name? Let's call him Sly!" Buddy excitedly replied.

CHAPTER 2

New School

Buddy had gone through this before. His first day of school was always nerve-wracking, and he tried to keep to himself. His rules were to avoid eye contact and dress conservatively. As he entered the back of the school grounds, he heard kids cheering.

"Bulldog, you're going to lose again!"

"Bulldog lost!"

As Buddy approached the crowd of students, they started to chant, "Choo, choo for the A-Train! Alvin and Raging Bull! Raging Bull! For Big E Eric!"

Huffing and puffing, a smaller boy with freckles pulled out his inhaler and put it in his mouth. He sat down on the bench Buddy was standing on to watch the race. He inhaled a deep breath.

"Hey, what's this all about?" Buddy asked with a curious look.

"Speed Racer Crown, the race that names the fastest kid in the school. A-Train never loses and is seldom challenged!" He looked at Buddy. "My name is Bulldog. You the new kid?"

"I'm Buddy."

Bulldog held out his hand. "Good to meet you, Buddy," he said with a smirk.

"You too," said Buddy. "How do you challenge A-Train?"

"Not that easy. He usually seeks the person out. Gym class, after practice, et cetera," replied Bulldog. "You play any sports? Let me guess, wrestling or cross country?"

Buddy was about to put his head down but remembered his dad's words from earlier. In a soft voice he said, "Football. I play football. My position is quarterback."

Bulldog gave him a fist bump. "That's what's up! But not at this school. That is A-Train's position," Bulldog replied confidently. "My dad told me that your dad is the new coach at Salem College. You must move around a lot," Bulldog said.

"Yeah, constantly. It's been hard," Buddy replied.

"We move around too. My dad is in the Navy and is constantly gone. I have friends all over the country," Bulldog boasted. Bulldog saluted with a serious look on his face. "Someday I will follow in my dad's footsteps. He is my hero," Bulldog said.

Bulldog then saw a football sticking out of Buddy's backpack. He took it out and brushed off the dust. Tossing the ball to Buddy, he said, "Let's see what you got!"

Buddy looked at him as if he was crazy. Bulldog burst into a full sprint and juked through the crowd. At this point all the attention shifted to Bulldog and Buddy. Buddy clenched the ball and heaved it with all his might high into the air.

Bulldog was thirty yards out, and it sailed over his head, surprising Buddy. A trail of light surrounded the ball, and there were sparkles visible to Buddy but no one else. Bulldog couldn't believe his eyes.

Buddy slowly made his way into the main office thinking about what he just saw. He pinched his arm to see if he was dreaming.

A-Train grabbed Bulldog by the arm hard. "Who was that?"

"That was the new kid," said Bulldog.

"He will be my backup," said A-Train.

Three stories high, Coach Mike had a bird's eye view. He was the most successful coach in the program's history and was excited to install the "West Coast" offense.

Buddy walked down the hall to the main office with white knuckles from squeezing his backpack straps. He entered the main office. A younger woman with blonde hair and a big smile stood behind the desk. Her badge said *Ms. Gloria*.

A girl similar to Buddy's age, tall and lean, with long brown wavy hair and big green eyes stood by the door.

"Good morning," Ms. Gloria said. "You must be Buddy!"

"That is correct," Buddy replied.

"Welcome to our school," she said as she went into the file cabinet. "This is your class schedule. In addition I included information about our school programs. Fall sports start tomorrow. I heard you have quite the arm."

"Thank you," Buddy said smiling.

"Buddy, this is Gianna," Ms. Gloria said. "She will bring you to your first class."

Gianna was shy but smiled with excitement.

Both of them left the office. The halls were crowded as all the students arrived. Gianna walked with so much confidence that it immediately caught Buddy's attention.

"Hey, G," said a taller, muscular boy standing next to his locker. He was rocking a *Salem Witches Football* T-shirt. "You ready to kick some bomb field goals today?"

"Been practicing all summer, Big E," Gianna replied. "I hope you worked on your hands!"

As they walked down the hall Buddy noticed kids staring at him. He overheard someone say, "Did you see the arm on him?"

They stopped at Buddy's locker then went to his first class, which was history with Ms. Frost.

When they arrived at Buddy's class, Gianna asked, "Will I see you at practice tomorrow? I'm the kicker."

"Not sure. I heard A-Train plays quarterback, and that's the position I play," Buddy replied.

"A-Train is fast but not the best at throwing," Gianna said laughing. "Coach loves to make things competitive, and we are going to have a good team this year."

Buddy quietly walked into class and sat at an empty desk. He looked in the back of the room, and A-Train was giving him a prizefighter staredown.

CHAPTER 3

Paper Route

The next day, Buddy awoke with his Boxer puppy, Sly, playing on his bedroom floor. He had a note attached to the bandanna around his neck.

> *Son, the athletic director of Salem College was able to secure a paper route job for you. It covers historic Salem and is one day a week before school. Sly could use the exercise!*
>
> *Love, Dad.*

He opened up the additional sheet of paper that was enclosed with the letter, and it was a map with all the delivery addresses: *PS, Follow the Heritage Trail and pick up my order from the shoe shop.*

A delivery tote bag filled with papers was neatly placed at the front door. It had a shoulder strap, and the words *Salem Times* were written across the bag.

The first stop was the Salem Witch Museum, which neigh

-bored his apartment. The mail slot on the door was jammed, and while he was trying to insert the paper, the door sprung open and Sly ran in.

The museum sat in complete darkness, which spooked Buddy. He built up his courage and sprinted after Sly. But he had no luck. Sly's brindle coat blended in with the rugs.

Moments later, he heard barking and growling. Entering another wing of the museum, he spotted Sly in front of a granite statue of a witch.

"Bad boy!" Buddy said as they ran out of the museum. Looking back, Buddy saw a curtain on the second floor pulled back. A wizard of a man stared out the window. It must have been Kurtin Drapes, the owner of the museum and commissioner of the middle school football league. He was known for being one of the coldest men in the city. Buddy told Sly that he would be witch's stew the next time he entered that museum.

Crossing the street, he paused and looked up at the Roger Conant statue. He was the founder of Salem, and Buddy saluted him as he passed. Then a familiar voice called his name. Gianna appeared walking a little dog. Buddy squatted down to pat him and noticed his collar read *Yogi*. While he was patting Yogi he asked Gianna if she would like to join him and help him figure out his way around Salem. Since she was born in Salem, Gianna knew the city like the back of her hand, and she was eager to be his tour guide.

Then they walked by the Hawthorne Hotel, Salem's most well-known hotel. Flags representing different countries hung in front, and tourists with European accents waited for cabs. One dropped a book, and Buddy picked it up and read the words

House of Seven Gables. Buddy handed it to an attractive lady, who smiled and pinched his cheek. Buddy's face turned bright red, and Gianna laughed.

Next they headed up Essex Street. His next stop was the Peabody Essex Museum. Buddy took a paper out and handed it to a worker in exchange for a shiny silver dollar. Buddy felt like he was living inside of a history book, his favorite subject. Surprisingly, it was Gianna's as well.

He grabbed a snack and sat at the East India Square Fountain. He dropped a coin in and made a wish. Sly barked at his reflection in the water while Yogi jumped in the fountain in an attempt retrieve the coin. They both laughed at the same time and agreed he would be good on the football field.

On this route, one of the spots was Bewitched. Buddy thought this was a unique shop, with all different trinkets. He got spooked after a toy witch shot down a zip line. The owner smiled at Sly and gave him a Salem witches bandanna.

Wicked Books was his next stop. He wanted to buy a book with some of his earnings. Gianna waited outside on a bench with both dogs. Skimming through the history section, he stumbled across an old, mysterious book about spells that seemed to glimmer when he opened it. Dropping a few dollars on the counter, he slipped it into his paper route bag and quickly exited the store.

From there they cut through an old cemetery. Buddy noticed the dates on the faded stones. Slowly walking across a path, he entered the Witchcraft Memorial. Sly broke away and ran in. Buddy chased after him thinking, *I really have to train this dog.*

Walking down Liberty Street, Buddy made his way to Gagnon Shoes, where he picked up his dad's loafers, which shined like the morning sun, and handed off a paper. Sly was given a milk bone and wagged his tail.

Their next stop was Boston Chimney. An older gentleman named Mr. Ron greeted them at the door and happily gave Buddy a hometown welcome to Salem and tossed him a miniature red plastic football. *The beauty of being young*, Mr. Ron thought. He had a magical twinkle in his eye, and it caught both of their attentions.

Next was the Cheese Shoppe of Salem. The cobblestone streets and architecture of the shop brought him back in time. The owner, Mr. Endicott, tipped his hat and smiled as he accepted the paper.

Coming up to the Friendship, a real-size replica of an eighteenth-century ship, Buddy stopped to take in the beauty of the scenery. Sailboats filled the harbor. An artist sat by the Custom House working on his painting.

His eyes shifted to the map, and he made his way into Witch Way Gifts.

The House of Seven Gables was a place he admired, and he looked forward to visiting this iconic landmark. Gianna excitedly said, "It has a secret passageway. Rumor has it that Hawthorne left a map to a hidden treasure." Buddy thought if he found that treasure, they would never have to move again.

Their final stop was Ye Olde Pepper Candy Companie. The smell of candy infused the air. Pushing the door open, he could sense it was time for breakfast as his stomach let off a growl so loud Sly barked. Mr. Bob greeted Buddy with a grin, eager to get his paper. He handed Buddy a bag of goodies. "Welcome to the neighborhood, my boy!" Looking at Gianna, he winked and said, "I see you have a tour guide." He handed her some chocolates.

Parting ways, Buddy asked Gianna if he could sit with her at lunch. Gianna swore Buddy to secrecy and told him she had to go into Boston for a doctor's appointment to see a specialist. Buddy did not think Gianna even looked sick, but he did not want to upset his new friend.

As he made his way home, he thought, *My dad had a really good idea with this paper route. I'm getting to know my way around this place pretty fast.* Salem seemed like a magical place.

CHAPTER 4

Practice Makes Perfect

The following day, Buddy awoke and immediately looked at his goals.

1.) Salem starting QB
2.) Make friends
3.) Be nice to everyone I meet
4.) Always try my hardest
5.) Dream big
6.) Do my chores
7.) Repeat 1 through 6

On the foot of his bed he had a note from his dad. He read it as he made his way to the equipment room.

Son, have a great day at school and good luck with your first practice. High energy, but most importantly have fun. I love you.

Dad!

Buddy walked anxiously into the equipment room. Before he could step on the field, team weigh-ins were required. Buddy and Gianna were clearly the smallest kids in the room.

As A-Train walked past, he towered over him by six inches. Giggling, he said, "Little boy, can you even see over the line of scrimmage?"

Most of the team burst into laughter. Gianna stood up and loudly yelled, "At least he does not throw like a wimp." The locker room laughed and let out an "Ohhhh!"

Coach Mike made his entrance and reminded the kids of the team bullying rules. Coach Mike was a tan, small, defined man who was always looked up to as a father figure. He loved the game and walked with passion and pride. *Salem Witches* stood out on his hooded sweatshirt.

The weight requirements were between 80 and 135 pounds. Every player took turns weighing in as Coach Howie and Coach Bruce recorded the results. Bulldog 85 pounds, Big E 125, Gus 134.5. The final two were A-Train and Buddy. Buddy thought to himself, *I hope my big breakfast is going to help here.*

A-Train stepped on the scale, and it read 137 pounds.

Before Buddy stepped on, he bumped his bag, and the sparkles he saw the day before were trailing from his ball once again, and no seemed to notice it. He nervously got on the scale, and was surprised to see he met the requirement. One more thing getting him closer to his goal. Buddy started to question whether he should have taken that ball.

Coach Mike's voice got loud as he said, "It's not the size of the dog but the fight of the dog," and he let out a growl, showing his teeth. "Welcome to our football family, Buddy."

Coach Mike blew his whistle, signaling the team to the

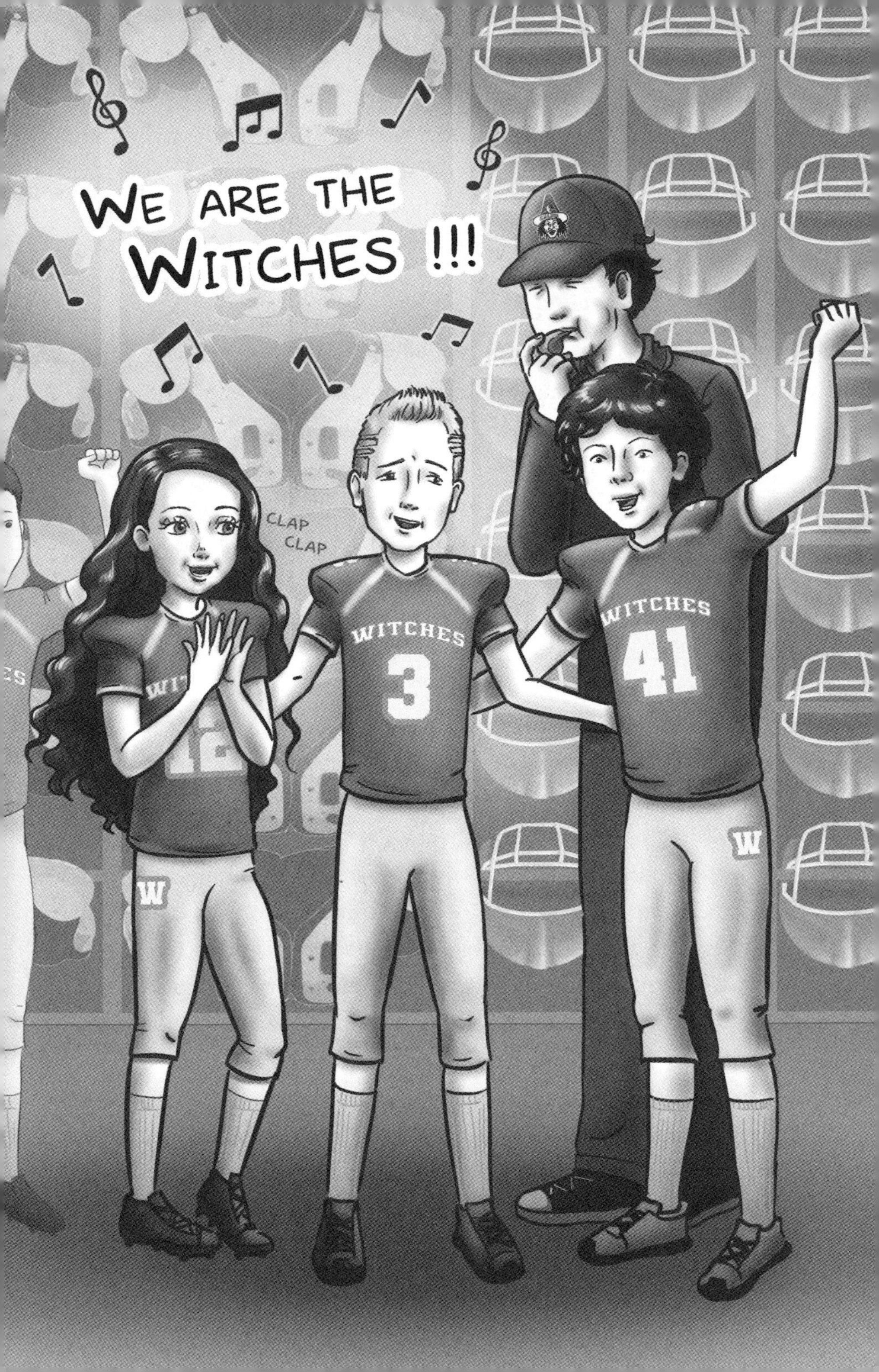

WE ARE THE WITCHES !!!
CLAP CLAP
WITCHES
3
WITCHES
41

practice field. "Hey team! How about giving Buddy a proper welcome!"

Each player started to clap twice and then banged their thigh pads in sync. "We are the Witches, the mighty, mighty Witches. Everywhere we go, people want to know who we are, so we tell them! We are the Witches! The mighty, mighty Witches!"

Coach Mike said, "Breakdown!" and the team roared.

"The season kickoffs are Saturday, and if we want to compete with Lynn or Beverly we have a great deal of work to do," Coach Mike said. "Hard work on three! One, two, three..."

"Hard work!" all of them yelled.

A-Train led the team onto the field. Coach Mike grabbed Buddy and handed him a playbook. "It's a new season, and we are installing the West Coast offense. Run and gun! Pay attention to my hand signals. Help her carry the water."

Coach's daughters Giulietta, who they called Little G, and Siena dragged the water cooler on the field. Little G proudly wore a big Salem football jersey with a side knot that tailored the jersey to fit. Her ponytail was always tied to perfection. She was a vocal little girl who was stronger and faster than most boys. They always begged her dad to let her play. Siena tried to keep pace with her big sister.

A-Train was a natural leader and picked up the playbook quickly.

Coach Mike tapped Buddy on the shoulder. "Tell A-Train to go to running back and have Big E run a fade ball like he was late for supper."

"Yes, Coach!" He buckled up his chinstrap and bolted onto the field carrying his ball from the basement.

A-Train shook his head with frustration running over his face.

"Set, go!" Buddy yelled and clapped his hands.

Buddy, light on his feet, took a three-step drop. Big E, his wide receiver, was twenty-five yards downfield with separation. Buddy tossed a tight spiral high in the air, and with a trail of light and sparkles following the ball it landed right in Big E's hands.

Buddy started to believe the ball had magical powers.

Coach Mike blew his whistle then walked over to Buddy and gave him a high five.

Big E jogged back, gasping for air.

Gianna added, "Great throw, new kid!"

"Appreciate it," Buddy replied. A sensation of joy swept through his body. "Gianna, did you see light trailing the ball?"

"No, just a really tight spiral and a witch on a broomstick," Gianna said, laughing. As she turned away to walk off towards home, Buddy saw that Gianna kind of limped. He wondered if Gianna had been injured during practice. If so, she'd said nothing about it. She must have been one tough kid.

Later on that evening, Buddy sat at his desk in his room with his history book open on one side and the playbook on the other. He never really understood playbooks, but for some reason this one was coming really easily for him. He was beginning to wonder why and if there were going to be consequences for all this magic.

Knowing the weigh-in was tomorrow night, he drank two glasses of chocolate milk and ate four of Owa's gluten free chocolate chip cookies.

He turned the light off and grabbed a flashlight out of his drawer. Then he reached into his bag and pulled out the mysterious spell book. Skimming through each page, he recognized the exact football he had found from a picture in the book. The year 1914 was highlighted.

The spell read, "He who touches the ball will develop special athletic powers. The thunder in the sky and snowfall will bring a pleasant surprise in a cold night's sky. Merchant."

Feeling a sense of excitement and fear at the same time, he wrapped the book in a blanket and pushed it far under his bed.

When he heard his dad making his way up the stairs he quickly jumped into bed.

That night, Buddy dreamed of the book, the ball, and the spell. When he woke up he had an idea. What if touching the ball somehow protected every person who touched it? He decided to start a tradition where every player would touch the ball before each game.

CHAPTER 5

Friday Night Magic

The team entered the locker room one by one for the official weigh-in. It was the first home game of the season, against the Lynn Tigers. The concrete stands were filled to capacity.

A-Train was watching his weight, as Coach Mike constantly fed him fruit salads. Buddy, on the other hand, struggled to gain weight and always seemed to have a problem with weight requirements, but that appeared to all be gone now. He was questioning the ball and what was inside the spell book.

A-Train was first on the scale and weighed in at 136 pounds. Coach Mike tried a second attempt, which Commissioner Kurt Drapes squashed. Buddy was next on the scale, and he confidently stepped on. The weight fluctuated and yet again met the requirement.

How is this happening so easily? Buddy thought.

Kurt Drapes announced A-Train was ineligible to play for a weight violation.

Coach Mike tossed Buddy the ball. "Lead us, young man."

Buddy took the ball and held it out. He looked into the eyes of each teammate and said loudly, "Everyone, touch the ball for good luck, and we will not be defeated." The tradition was born.

As he ran onto the field, Buddy spotted his dad, Owa, and sister in the crowd. Sophia jumped up and down when she saw him.

The Witches lost the coin toss and kicked off. The defense forced the Tigers to punt. Buddy's adrenaline was pumping through his body. Bulldog, the offense, and Buddy sprinted onto the field.

"Jet toss on one!" Buddy called. Big E moved to running back.

Buddy tossed the ball to Big E, who ran through the hole. Buddy was the lead blocker and cut the defensive end, giving Big E running room for a first down.

They huddled up as Buddy got the signal. Coach Mike had taped all the plays inside Buddy's game jersey just in case he forgot any of them.

In the huddle, Buddy gave the play, "Big E, motion left, which will leave Bulldog on an island. Gus, the stout offensive lineman resembling a bowling ball."

"I don't think Bulldog can swim." The team laughed.

"Bulldog, run like it's time for supper! I'm looking for you," Buddy said.

Lining up over center, Buddy motioned Big E, who took the linebacker with him.

"Set... go! Go!" Buddy shouted out.

Bulldog took an inside release, surprising the defensive back who attempted to jam him on the line. Buddy looked left and took the safety over. Buddy tossed a beautiful tight spiral into the night air, and a trail of light and sparkles followed ball. Bulldog caught it and raced into the end zone.

Buddy pointed up to the sky, thinking of his mom, but at

that moment he realized he had magical powers. He was a football wizard.

The Witches scored six points for the touchdown. Gianna raced onto the field to kick the extra point. Buddy, who was the holder, got into position. "Please do not kick my fingers," Buddy said.

"I usually only do it once a game and will try not to," Gianna confidently replied.

The extra point is worth one more point, and it was good! Witches 7, Tigers 0 after the first quarter.

The Tigers' running back Kam Green led his team back. He had a great combo of size, strength, and speed, but a short leash, which often got him penalized. The defense stopped them in the red zone.

Throughout the game, Buddy threw two more touchdown passes followed by a trail of light and sparkles, and Gianna made all her extra point kicks. Ballet helped her develop a strong leg, and she celebrated every kick she made with a pirouette. The final whistle blew, and the scoreboard read *Witches 21, Tigers 7.*

CHAPTER 6

The Race

Buddy continued his weekly routine, and he considered his paper route time to reflect with Sly. Gianna continued to join him, and they both enjoyed each other's company. Their first win against the Tigers proved they were a tough team as the Tigers went on to dominate their next three opponents.

His dad's college team was undefeated.

On the way to school, a kid who was known to be one of A-Train's friends approached Buddy and Bulldog. He handed Buddy a note that read, *I am back and ready to challenge you. Let's start with a race, small fry. Tomorrow in front of the school.* The messenger watched Buddy read the letter and said, "This is from A-Train," and he pointed his finger into Buddy's small chest.

Buddy was very intimidated. He was starting to wonder if he should even bother to play on the team. He had no other choice but to stand up to the challenge, but even Bulldog did not think he had a chance.

It was a rough afternoon, and nothing seemed to be going his way.

When Buddy got home, there was a package on his bed. He had no idea what it could be. It wasn't his birthday, but the timing was perfect since he was having a bad day.

It was a box with a note:

> *This is something you might need. As you know, your mom always wanted you to have nice things.*

Buddy looked up at his goals, and he knew he had to stand up to the challenge. He tore the red bow and wrapping paper off. *Adidas, size 5* was written on the box.

He opened up the box slowly, savoring the surprise. There they were, the limited Adidas Turbo's. Goosebumps shot through every part of Buddy's body. He had a half smile as a tear rolled down his cheek.

As he slipped them on, Buddy could feel his body transforming at that very moment. His strides got longer as he walked, his confidence was soaring, and he was ready to challenge the bully.

The entire school filed in to watch. Students whispered, "He doesn't have a chance." A-Train was in the zone warming up.

Gianna walked up to Buddy. "You do not have to do this. Coach Mike makes the decisions on who plays."

Buddy smiled and walked past her. "I need to stand up to him." Gianna was surprised by Buddy's newfound confidence.

Buddy and A-Train both lined up as a path was cleared and fifty yards marked off.

Bulldog pulled out an old whistle. "The sound of the whistle means go!"

A-Train's friend who delivered the message pulled it from Bulldog's hands. "I will do the honors."

A-Train stared Buddy down. Towering over him, he did not

even realize the road Buddy had traveled and how mentally tough he was.

Most of the students started to chant, "Choo! Choo! Choo! Choo!" in favor of A-Train. A small amount of the students shouted out, "Buddy Bee fly! Buddy Bee fly!"

Bulldog yelled out, "Hey, Buddy. I love those new kicks, old school, baby!" Buddy chuckled at the expression on his friend's face. The tension was broken.

The whistle blew, and A-Train accelerated out using his long stride and power. He was clearly in favor to win. Buddy stayed low and relaxed, pumping his arms.

They were in a deadlock for forty yards, but Buddy pushed harder and nudged ahead. He crossed the finish line with the victory!

Coach Mike's office overlooked the finish line. *Looks like my decision is made. The bumble bee has flown!* Coach Mike thought.

The students started to chant, "Buddy Bee! Buddy Bee!"

Buddy walked through the crowd giving fist bumps. For the first time at a school the students actually knew his name.

The toughest opponent was next on their schedule. The Witches were facing a fierce Beverly Panthers team, who was also their archrival. "The rivalry started in 1890 at the Salem Commons," Coach Mike informed the team.

"A-Train and Buddy, I want you both in my office before practice," said Coach Mike.

Coach Mike's office was a shrine of team photos and motivational quotes all over his walls. Not an inch of wall space was left. He volunteered for years developing boys and girls, instilling confidence, character, and discipline in them. He was determined to win his first league championship.

Both boys sat side by side and did not acknowledge each other. Coach Mike always stressed to the team that football was the ultimate team sport.

"There is clearly friction between you both. A-Train, you're moving to running back, and Buddy, you're our quarterback. Glad you guys made my decision easier with the race. Everyone's ego needs to be left at the door," Coach Mike stated in a stern voice. "Now shake on this and remember your commitment to the team."

They both looked at each other uncomfortably. This was the last thing Buddy wanted to do.

"One more thing. Team bonding is the key to building character and chemistry. Gianna gave me a great idea. She will conduct tomorrow's practice at the ballet studio she attends."

Both players giggled. "You got it, coach!" they replied.

Buddy thought to himself, *Another challenge. I hope they don't expect us to wear a leotard too.*

CHAPTER 7

Ballet School

The ballet studio was not far from school. Some of the team rode their bikes. Buddy, Big E, and Bulldog walked.

Each player wore practice pants and a T-shirt, and borrowed ballet shoes from the studio. A beautiful fifteenth-century Italian Renaissance painting hung in the room. Coach Mike lined up the team in groups of five. Ms. Krista, Gianna's mom, played classical music on the piano.

Gianna timed her entrance to the beat of the music, surprising a lot of her teammates by her grace. Her bun was precise. She wore tights, a crop top, and a leotard.

She put the team through the five positions. Players' giggles filled the room, but as the movements got more intense, the talking stopped.

Gianna had Coach Mike demonstrate a pirouette in ballet shoes, which the team found funny. The team attempted to try one, but they all fell over like dominos. Gus started spinning in the wrong direction. Bulldog faked a cramp.

Buddy seemed to be the only kid who understood the technique of ballet. The other players seemed confused and lost in the steps, but he felt as if he had done the steps before. With his

football in his bag, he felt very confident and brave.

Towards the end of class, Gianna performed three perfect pirouettes in a row and four fouette turns. The team just stood there amazed. Gianna called out two volunteers. You could hear a pin drop until Coach Mike decided to select Buddy and A-Train. Bulldog hid in the back.

"If these two can pass the test, we are done for the day and pizza is on me. If not, conditioning on the field," Coach Mike stated.

Both players stood a few feet apart from each other. "Please get in the first position. Well done," Gianna said. Next she had them leap across the floor. A-Train missed his footing and tumbled over onto the floor.

Buddy was synchronized, and as he moved he could see the sparkles shoot off his feet. Declaring Buddy the winner, Gianna asked him if he had taken classes before.

Coach Mike smiled as he felt a bond being created. Bulldog had a bigger smile when the Panini Pizzeria delivery boy brought in twelve pizzas!

As the team left the studio, Buddy asked Gianna to come over to his house.

Buddy couldn't get home fast enough to get the book from underneath his bed to share with Gianna and learn more about his newfound power. He was curious, and the fear of the spell left him.

Buddy ran into his room, grabbed the book, and waited for Gianna out front as he watched crowds of people visit the Salem Witch Museum.

Not too long after, Gianna showed up on her bicycle. Gianna thought he wanted to talk about football. Buddy did not know where to begin.

Before he showed her anything, Buddy swore her to secrecy. As he opened up the book, he told her about what he saw every time he threw the ball: running at great speed to beat A-Train and throwing the ball further and with more accuracy than he ever had before.

Gianna had lived in the city her entire life and had been waiting for a moment like this. "You were not even here for a day and walked into something like this?" Gianna excitedly said. As Gianna slowly read the spell her eyes got wider and wider.

They spent the next few hours reviewing the book and trying to figure it all out.

CHAPTER 8
No Backing Down

Buddy sat on the front stairs of his house as Sly wrestled in the crisp autumn leaves. He proudly wore his Salem Football hoodie with #3 embroidered on the arm. He chose the number because it was his mom's birthday month.

He enjoyed his new school and felt like he had an extended family with the football team. Being around them made him happy, and he had a best friend in Gianna.

When Buddy stepped into the apartment, he was so excited to tell Owa and his dad about his day. He could hear Owa and Sophia speaking in her room.

Buddy found his dad sitting on the back porch with a letter opened in front of him. His face was like concrete. He pointed, indicating for Buddy to have a seat next to him.

Buddy could sense something was off. As he slowly sat down, Buddy held his breath.

"How was your day?" Dad asked.

Buddy smiled. "Interesting," he said, sitting back in the chair.

Dad took a deep breath. "Do you like your team and coaches?"

"Yeah they are great, never played so well!" Buddy replied.

Dad took a deep breath and paused as he handed Buddy the letter.

Buddy's feet were glued to the floor. His big blue eyes suddenly became smaller, and tears filled his vision.

"Son, I am sorry," Dad replied. "This is a great opportunity. It's a better life for you and Sophia."

Buddy felt like he fell off a cliff.

"When do we need to move by?" Buddy asked. At this point Buddy was gripping the bottom of his chair.

After a long pause, his dad said, "Soon."

Buddy's mouth was dry. His head started to hurt. "Will I get to finish the season?" Buddy was so frustrated.

Dad's eyes looked into the dark sky. "I explained the situation to Coach Mike."

Buddy stood up with tears streaming down his cheeks; disappointment ran through his body. "How can you do this to me again? To us. Life is so unfair."

Grandma Owa stood in the doorway holding Sophia close and attempted to console Buddy.

Buddy avoided her. "Leave me alone. I just need time!"

He grabbed Sly, his bag with the ball, and the spell book. Slamming the door, he ran into the night. The city was preparing for Haunted Happenings.

His mom was on his mind. Halloween was one of her favorite holidays. Looking up into the stars, he was certain his mother would have never allowed the family to move again.

He wondered if he could use the magic of the football to help his family stay in Salem.

CHAPTER 9

Full Moon

Buddy ran across the frosted grass on the Commons and sat down on a bench. It was a cold, damp night, and he was ruining his new shoes. Numbness filled his fingertips. Buddy wanted to believe that this was a bad dream. The moon was full and reflected off the ocean. Stars filled the sky. Sly sensed his pain as he rested his head on Buddy's leg, letting out a big sigh. Removing a bandanna from his pocket, he wiped the tears off his face.

Thoughts of quitting the team ran through his head. *I am going to let my teammates down*, Buddy thought. A light was coming from his bag. He removed the mysterious spell book. Buddy was desperate to try anything to convince his dad to stay.

A hand gently rested on his back, surprising Buddy but not fazing Sly as his ears went back. He quickly slammed the book shut. His dad sat down next to him and put his arm around him.

"I wonder how many people have traveled these waters." Dad smiled as he looked out at the boats in the water. "Your grandfather traveled by steamboat from Italy for thirty days to chase the American Dream. He was a brave man who had to make tough decisions," Dad preached.

Buddy sat still, absorbing his dad's words. "Do you think he was scared?" Buddy replied.

"To some degree, yes," Dad expressed.

Dad could sense the grief it was causing him. "My goal is to give you the best possible life. I promised your mom that. Friday's game is going to be exciting. Your team needs you. Coach Mike is so proud of you guys."

Looking deep into his son's eyes, he said with confidence, "Live in the moment, son. We always land on our feet." Buddy truly wanted to believe him, but a part of him could not bring himself to do it.

They had to go home now. Owa was going to be worried sick, and Sophia needed to pick up her Halloween costume. Sly wagged his tail and barked at the ducks in the water.

Dad walked slowly with his arm wrapped around Buddy's shoulder. "We will figure this thing out, son," Dad softly said.

A shooting star streaked across the sky. Buddy glanced at his dad and wondered if he saw it too.

CHAPTER 10

Halloween

Sly's wet kisses awoke Buddy from a deep sleep. His desk calendar read October 31st. A sense of excitement came over him. One day before the big game against Beverly.

Buddy laid out his football gear, which was a tradition he did before his games. When he realized he forgot his ball in the locker room, a little panic ran through him.

Halloween in Salem brought everyone back to his or her youth. Peeking his head out the window, he could see people dressed in seventeenth-century costumes fill the streets. The Salem Witch Museum resembled a haunted house.

Sophia, dressed as a witch with her face painted, galloped with a broomstick. As always, her energy level was high, and she was impatiently waiting for Halloween in her new city.

"I have a letter from a witch for you. Don't worry, it is not a spell being put on you. It's from a good witch." Smiling, she turned and cartwheeled away. The envelope had a drawing of witch on a broomstick carrying a football.

Coach Mike informed me that it is an annual tradition for football players to go trick-or-treating together as a team. Meet at the Commons at five o'clock!

Love, Dad.

Gianna showed up with eye black, but some of the players were hesitant to allow her to apply it to their faces.

Buddy stepped up and said, "I'll go first. I trust you since you haven't kicked my fingers." Buddy smiled.

She put the eye black under his eyes and made a line going down his noise. Bulldog was next, and Gianna surprised him by drawing a set of whiskers.

A-Train loved warriors, and Gianna was able to show her artistic side. Even Coach Mike got into the spirit and put eye black under his eyes.

The team went in and out of witchcraft stores and souvenir shops, and their bags were filling up. Hay bales covered the sides of the road, and corn stalks were tied to the lampposts with orange and black ribbon. This reminded Buddy of his school colors, red and black.

Buddy was excited to visit some of his paper route customers. He heard Gagnon Shoes gave out bags of Swedish Fish, which he knew were Coach Mike's favorite. He thought it would be cool to get some for him.

Mr. Ron dropped gift cards to Dairy Witch into the players' bags. As the owner of Boston Chimney, during the Christmas season he would make sure the chimneys were clean for Santa's delivery. He placed his hands on Buddy and Gianna's shoulders

and said, "Looks like your team is a good one. Feel the magic in the air." Then he took off his cap, and sparkles flew off it.

Mr. Endicott at the Cheese Shoppe of Salem had a surprise for the team; he was handing out blocks of Red Witch cheese. He winked at Buddy when it was his turn in line and placed an extra piece in his bag. "One for Sly."

The final stop of the evening was Ye Olde Pepper. You could smell the vanilla in the air. The candy store was softly lit and had a haunted theme to it. Buddy saved up his paper route money to buy a special treat.

The owners Mr. Bob and Ms. Jackie dressed in costumes. Large chocolate bars were handed out to each of the players. Bulldog was about to receive his treat when a clown popped up from underneath a table, frightening him and causing him to scream and stumble.

The laughs from the team got louder and louder as Coach Mike removed the mask!

Buddy soaked it all up. He felt he had a strong connection to his team and was having the time of his life. Part of him wanted to detach himself from the team, but he felt this bond could never be broken. He felt magical!

Meanwhile, in the Witches' locker room, the Beverly captain, Cal, decided to pay a visit while the team was out trick-or-treating. He closely went through their things. He took out his cell phone and took photos of several pages of the playbook before he got nervous and remembered what he really came for. He then began his search for the magical football, and he found it in Buddy's locker.

CHAPTER 11

A Dilemma

The wind howled outside of the locker room as rain grazed the windows. Buddy eyed his playbook. Echoes from the Beverly locker room got louder as game time approached. Kickoff was less than thirty minutes away. Buddy's dad's words played in his head, "Live in the moment, son!"

Buddy was staring at a photo. Standing next to him, Gianna could sense something was wrong, so she asked, "Who's that, Buddy?"

Buddy hesitantly said, "My mom. She passed away, and I miss her so much."

"She's beautiful." But Gianna knew there was something else too.

"My dad got offered a new job and is moving us to the Midwest soon."

"I am so sorry, Buddy." Placing the kicking tee on the bench, Gianna sat beside him. "I guess we do not have any other choice but to win tonight."

Buddy, grinning, said, "You're right."

He went to grab the ball out of his locker, but it was gone. Buddy always kept it in the same spot, the back of the locker in his Salem College football gym bag. Buddy was panicking and searched the entire locker room. No ball. "What am I going to do?" Buddy said to himself.

Oh no, he thought. *What about our pre-game tradition?* If the ball was truly magical, they were in big trouble.

Gianna looked at him and said, "Where's the ball?" Nervously, Buddy replied that it was missing.

Coach Mike led the team onto the field. The stadium was packed. The announcer made it clear that the winner would most likely be league champs.

The conditions were wet. Buddy hated wet games, as he had trouble gripping a wet ball. The Witches lost the coin toss and would kick off. The Panthers received the kick and returned it seventy-seven yards for the score.

"Touchdown Panthers!" The announcer's voice echoed through the stadium.

Buddy fumbled the first offensive snap, and he walked off the field with his head down.

"Chin up!" Coach Mike yelled. "Lot of football left!"

On the Panthers' next possession, their quick running back took the toss and broke up the field for a big game.

On the next play, Coach Mike signaled a blitz. Gus, the defensive leader, had the 'D' fired up. The perfect offensive play was called for an all-out blitz. Using a screen pass, the quarterback lobbed a pass over Bulldog's head. The Panthers caught the ball and raced up the field. A-Train had the angle but ran out of gas.

The referee signaled, "Touchdown Panthers!"

Coach Mike approached each defensive player jogging off the field with a fist bump. "Eye of the tiger, boys." Looking at Gianna, he added, "Girls too!"

Buddy led the Witches' offense onto the field. "A-Train, we need to ride the train now," Buddy yelled out.

Buddy got under center. He looked so tiny the defense could not see him. "Set, go, hut! Hut!" A-Train took the handoff and burst through the hole, picking up a big gain and moving the chains. The crowd chanted, "Choo! Choo!"

The Witches continued to pound the football play after play, moving the ball into the red zone. They were eating a lot of the clock up.

Buddy read nine defenders in the box, which signaled a defensive blitz. He slapped the side of his left leg, which audibled for a quick swing pass to a wide-open A-Train. Buddy's pass fell incomplete.

Next play, they went back to the run game and a toss to A-Train. Big E delivered a vicious crack block, allowing A-Train to cross the goal line.

Gianna's extra point split the uprights and was good. High fives made their way around the Witches' sidelines.

The scoreboard read, *Panthers 14, Witches 7*, with less than two minutes left to play in the game. Buddy was concerned, as he knew they would need to pass the ball to win the game.

The Witches forced a fumble on the Panthers' next possession. Bulldog ran off the field jumping for joy, holding the football up that he recovered.

Coach Mike started yelling at Bulldog, "You play offense," and slapped him on the helmet. Bulldog sprinted back on the field.

The rain was pouring down. Buddy dried his hands off with the towel that hung from inside his waist.

"We need to utilize the clock and preserve time. Make sure

to run out of bounds. Fake bootleg pass on one. Ready, break!"

Buddy took the handoff and faked a bootleg. Just as he was going to get hit, he spun, avoiding the defender. A-Train quickly speeded up the field and was wide open in the end zone. Breaking several more tackles, he spotted A-Train. Planting his feet, he let the ball go. No trail of light followed... no sparkles. It traveled twelve yards, to the goal line. The ball went through A-Train's hands and hit a Panthers player's helmet, shooting into the air. Gus sprinted towards the goal line and caught the deflection. His momentum helped him into the end zone.

"Touchdown Witches!"

Gianna made her way onto the field, and she gave Buddy the signal. The ball snapped back in place, and as she went through her steps, her plant leg gave out. Gianna fell to the ground in serious pain. Buddy was frozen as the Panthers dove onto the ball. The referees blew the whistle, signaling the game was over.

Buddy's heart sank in his chest. The magic was gone. Gianna was down on the ground. Big-E's head dropped. Bulldog looked up into the stands for his dad, and there was no sign of him.

The scoreboard read *Panthers 14, Witches 13.*

Commissioner Kurt Drapes walked slowly over to the sideline. He approached Buddy and said, "Looks like the better team won. There is always next year!" Letting off a fake smile, he slowly walked away.

Buddy was in complete shock and dropped his head in disappointment. Gianna witnessed it all.

Coach Mike, ignoring Drapes completely, huddled his team up. "Boys and girls, I know your hearts hurt, but I am so proud of all you accomplished this season. Thanks for leaving it all on the field. Uniform turn-in is tomorrow. 'Team' on three. One, two, three... TEAM!"

As Buddy walked away with his head down, he saw Cal across the field. The Beverly captain was taunting him, waving the magic ball in the air. Buddy headed towards him, and Cal threw the ball on the ground, yelling, "You couldn't win without the magic ball?"

Buddy went over and picked it up and started to think about what Cal said. Was it all true? Were all of their wins because of this magic ball?

Gianna slowly limped off. Buddy ran up to her. "You okay?" Buddy said.

"My arthritis is acting up. It's just something I have to deal with. Dress warm and stay loose," Gianna responded.

CHAPTER 12
Ten-Yard Fight

Buddy lay in his bed as the streetlights peeked through his blinds, hitting him in the eyes like stadium lights. His desk was empty. Boxes were stacked for the movers. His goals and picture of his mom stood out on the blank walls.

Multiple acorns hit his window, catching his attention. He looked out, surprised to see Gianna. She signaled him to come down.

"You couldn't use a telephone?" Buddy asked.

"Your house phone isn't working," Gianna replied.

"Oh that's right, we're leaving shortly."

"Coach Mike called for a mandatory meeting," Gianna said.

Shortly after, Gianna and Buddy jumped onto their bikes and soon arrived at the locker room. Bulldog and Big E arrived late, huffing and puffing.

Coach Mike told the team to listen up. He pulled out a piece of paper from his coat. All eyes were glued on him.

To: Coach Mike,

*With a new rule change, I am advising you
that Lynn, Beverly, and the Witches all share
the same record. Please arrive at my office with
your captains tomorrow at 5 pm. A coin toss will
determine the league champions.*

Commissioner Kurtin Drapes

Voices got louder. Frustration with a sense of excitement filled the air. Coach Mike called up A-Train as captain. "Buddy, I would select you to join, but I realize you're leaving town shortly," Coach Mike said.

Whispers went around the team until a deep voice stated out loud, "He's not going anywhere." It was Buddy's dad.

Buddy nearly got whiplash from turning around so fast. "Really, Dad?"

"Background check is taking longer than expected," Dad stated.

Joy shot throughout Buddy's body as he realized he could continue to chase magical mystery.

"In that case," Coach Mike said, "Buddy, I am naming you captain as well."

Commissioner Drapes' office had papers everywhere and smelled of mothballs. The Lynn captains wore their team sweat-shirts. The Beverly captains wore their hoodies. Drapes handed each captain a shiny quarter. A-Train nodded for Buddy to grab the coin.

"Matching heads or tails play each other. Three of a kind,

and we play a tiebreaker ten-yard fight Friday night," Drapes informed them.

On the blow of the whistle, all three of the captains tossed their coins in the air.

Lynn captain Green stood over it. "Tails never fails," he said.

Beverly's coin spun and eventually landed flat. The Beverly captain Cal jumped up, shouting, "Tails, baby!"

The Witches' coin swayed back and forth before it rolled under a desk and disappeared. Or, at least everyone thought it did. Drapes handed him another coin, and it rolled about ten feet before collapsing. Buddy partially covered his eyes, afraid to look. It was tails.

Drapes grabbed his cane and hobbled over and examined each coin one by one. He paused, looking at the Witches. "I apologize, but you need to do it over, as your coin is not a quarter," Drapes stated.

Coach Mike's face filled with frustration, and he bit his bottom lip as he shook his head.

Buddy tossed it high in the air, and it felt like an eternity coming down. It bounced several times before it landed.

Everyone ran over to it. "Tails it is," Buddy said. A-Train gave him a fist bump. Drapes clenched his fist. Exiting the building, the entire Witches football team waited in suspense.

Coach Mike, with a frown on his face, said, "Apparently luck is on our side. We are playing in the tie breaker!"

Back up in Drapes' office, he shifted his foot, revealing the first coin Buddy tossed that was supposedly lost. Hidden under Drapes' foot, it read tails. "I despise those Witches," he said.

That Friday night, frigid temperatures froze the field. Snow was in the forecast. Buddy sat in front of his locker wiping the football down, wondering if this ball had lost any of its magic.

Hip-hop music filled the locker room air. Coach Mike drew plays on the blackboard. He had the team take a knee. "Family first, my teammates second, and myself third. I am so grateful to have all of you in my life."

Walking around to each player, Coach Mike looked them in the eyes and paused. "A-Train, thank you. Big E, thank you. Gus, thank you. Gianna, thank you. Bulldog, thank you. Buddy, thank you."

Gianna could tell how badly Buddy wanted to win. She approached him. "May I write something on your inner forearm?" Buddy smiled and nodded his head yes.

Gianna pulled out a black Sharpie and wrote MOM 'GENA' with an arrow pointing towards the sky. "Just in case you need a little inspiration," Gianna said.

Buddy smiled and handed Gianna hand warmers and an extra pair of socks. Gianna hugged Buddy appreciatively. Buddy remembered the spell, and an idea hit him.

"Come with me," he said to Gianna and headed towards a corner in the locker room. He leaned in and quietly asked her, "Do you remember the words of the spell?"

"I know every word by heart."

Buddy and Gianna locked eyes, and they both put their hands on the ball and nodded. Without saying a word to each other, they moved to the locker room door leading to the field. By now everyone's eyes were on them, and the room was silent. Buddy and Gianna held the ball up as an archway, and together they recited the spell: "He who touches the ball will develop special athletic powers. The thunder in the sky and snowfall will bring a pleasant surprise in a cold night's sky."

As the team rushed through the door, one by one they reached up to touch the ball. The team burst onto the field with Gianna and Buddy in the rear. As Gianna and Buddy's feet touched the field, a burst of thunder rolled across the sky, and it began to snow.

The Witches won the coin toss and got to advance to the next round. Each team would get one series on offense and would get the ball at the ten-yard line with four plays to score.

Beverly got the ball first and was stuffed on four straight plays.

On Lynn's ball, they scored, so they moved into the final. The running back took the toss and made his way into the end zone untouched.

The announcer said, "Beverly is now eliminated!"

Buddy and Big E threw their last warm-up pass. Time for some action!

Buddy looked at Gianna and gave her a thumbs up, signaling to her the magic was back.

The Tigers' running back sidestepped a blitzing linebacker and dove towards the pylon.

"Touchdown Lynn!" the referee shouted.

Buddy blew on his fingers before getting under center.

Buddy motioned Big E into trips right. Buddy faked the toss to A-Train and jolted up the sidelines. "Touchdown Witches!"

Lynn would answer immediately, as their quarterback floated a ball into the air. The wide receiver exploded up into the air, catching it over Big E. "Touchdown Tigers!"

Buddy called out the cadence. A-train went in motion left... "Set, go, hut!"

Big E took a hard step forward, and Buddy threw a dart for

a quick slip screen. The ball traveled with a familiar sparkling trail of magic. Big E pivoted left, breaking a tackle! "Touchdown Witches!"

Gianna was amazed when she saw the sparkles for the first time. Buddy smiled. His powers were back!

Coach Mike was pacing the sidelines, biting on his fingernails. The crowd was cheering and charged up.

The Witches got the blitz signal and forced a fumble that got kicked to the one-yard line, where Lynn recovered. The crowd was on their feet. Buddy zoned in, trying to stay warm.

Coach Mike signaled timeout. "A-Train, spy on the running back. Everyone knows he is getting the ball."

The Lynn quarterback faked the dive and tossed it to the running back. A-Train instantly shot through the A-gap and sprinted towards him, taking away his angle. He left his feet like a warrior, tackling him, but his momentum carried him forward to cross the goal line. Touchdown! The Lynn kicker missed the extra point.

The announcer said, "If the Witches score and convert the extra point, they will be crowned league champions."

On the first play, Buddy fumbled the snap and fell on it. Buddy immediately called another play. He tried to catch them off guard.

On the next play, Buddy got slammed to the ground. When the players cleared the area, Buddy's eyes were closed, and his knee was bloody. His dad stood from his seat and started making his way down to the field.

The Witches needed seventeen yards to win. Coach Mike signaled timeout and sprinted onto the field. "A-Train, warm your arm up. Buddy might be done." Coach Mike informed them.

A-Train took a knee next to Buddy and reached for his hand. Buddy's eyes finally opened. Coach Mike smiled and softly said to himself, "Thank you."

Buddy sat up and looked at his inner forearm. *MOM 'GENA'* was the remedy he needed, and he slowly and painfully rose to his feet.

He signaled to Gianna to grab his bag under the bench. Taking off his cleats, he replaced them with the Adidas Turbo's.

Coach signaled for A-Train to go in as quarterback, but Buddy said with such desire, "Coach, we need this. I need this!"

"Okay, Buddy. Go make it happen!" Their eyes met. *Witches Special.* "Tell A-Train now is his chance to throw the ball," Coach Mike said.

The referee signaled the teams to resume play.

As he limped onto the field, he noticed his dad on the sideline. His presence gave Buddy the extra inspiration to do what had to be done.

The entire crowd was on their feet cheering.

"A-Train, Witches Special, QB throwback pass." A-Train's eyes got as big as the midnight sky. "Line, we need max protection! Ready, break! 'A' sell the run."

Buddy glanced at the defense. He took the snap and tossed it to A-Train. Buddy ran faster than he ever ran before. As soon as A-Train let the ball go, he got blasted under the chin, breaking his chinstrap.

The ball soared high in the air as if time had stopped. The defender was running in stride with Buddy, and he pushed harder but lost the ball, the trail of light nearly blinding him.

The safety was closing in, and the ball hit his helmet. Sparkles flew and bounced up as Buddy launched himself in the

air. The ball hit the pylon in the back corner of the end zone.

Buddy extended his arm and caught it with one hand, cradling it in.

The referee shouted, "Touchdown!"

Gianna jogged onto the field, feeling achy all over. But she wasn't letting anything stop her. This was her fight, and she was determined to win. She also planned to help the team by kicking the best she could.

As he set the kicking tee, Buddy's eyes met hers. She nodded her head, and the ball snapped low, which resulted in bobbling the snap. With the football placed on the tee, pressure was coming from the defense. Within seconds she got the kick off, and as it started to hook wide left, a big gust of wind repositioned the football and carried it over the uprights. The ball flashed like lightning.

Gianna and Buddy jumped for joy. "The kick is good! The kick is good!" the announcer exclaimed loudly.

Snow started to fall from the night sky while thunder sounded in the sky. A thunder snowstorm! The magic spell happened!

The Witches won the championship!

Commissioner Drapes angrily made a dramatic exit.

Buddy pointed up to the sky and blew a kiss. The team rushed the field. A-Train bear-hugged Buddy.

The Witches' team huddled around Coach Mike as Little G, Gianna, and Bulldog got the water jug ready to pour over Coach.

Bulldog faked a cramp, falling to the ground. Coach Mike got on his knees to assist. The team timed it as Buddy, A-Train, and Gianna poured ice water on him, and Bulldog screamed, "Gotcha!" rolling out of the way at the last second. The whole

team burst into laughter.

Bulldog's dad approached him. They got in position and both saluted one another. Bulldog's dad smiled proudly and hugged his boy.

Buddy and his dad's eyes locked at midfield. Dad picked him up, congratulating him. Holding Sophia, he spoke to them both. "Looks like we found our forever home."

Before Dad could finish talking, Sophia leaped happily out of his arms and started to make snow angels with Little G. Not long afterwards, the entire team followed her lead.

- ON THE FIELD -

 PYLON - Orange markers in front and back of end zones that indicate a touchdown or out of bounds

EZ **END ZONE** - The scoring area at each end of the field between the end line and goal line

RZ **RED ZONE** - The area from the 20-yard line to the end zone at each end of the field

--- **GOAL LINE** - The chalked or painted line dividing the field of play from the end zone

GOAL POSTS - Y-shaped structure the ball must travel through to score an extra point or field goal

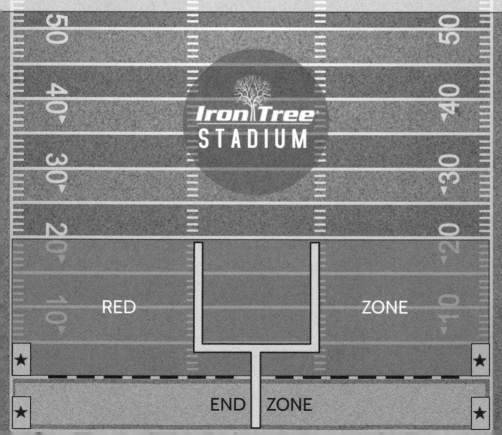

Glossary

A-gap – gap directly to each side of the center

Audible – when the quarterback uses cadence to change the play at the line of scrimmage

Blitz – when a non-defensive lineman is called upon to rush the passer

Bootleg pass – pass play in which the quarterback fakes handoff and sprints away in opposite direction

Chains – 0–10 yard marker that offense must cross to get a first down

Chinstrap – a strap buttoned to a helmet, which passes beneath the chin and holds the helmet in place

Completed pass – any time a pass attempt is caught by an offensive player. Passes are completed when the offensive player has gained possession of the ball by securing it with his hands or body and placing two feet down in the field of the play.

Crack block – a block by an offensive player, which they angle from the outside to the inside

Defensive blitz – a defensive player rushes the quarterback

Down – a period in which a play transpires. The team in possession of the ball has a limited number of downs (four downs to advance ten yards or more towards the goal line).

End zone – the scoring area on the field between the end line and goal line. There are two end zones on opposite sides of the field.

Extra point – kicking play after a touchdown is scored that is worth one point

Field goal – a kick that is worth three points if it goes between the goal posts

Fumble – a player loses the ball before hitting the ground

Goal line – the chalked or painted line dividing the end zone from the field of play. It is the line that must be broken in order to score a touchdown.

Incomplete pass – an attempt at a legal forward pass that hits the ground before a player on either team gains possession

Jet sweep – outside running play in which the ball carrier sprints in motion prior to receiving the football

Kicker – individual who kicks the ball to start play or kicks extra points and field goals

Linebacker – defensive player that aligns behind the defensive line

Lineman – (DL or OL) a defensive or offensive player that aligns at the line of scrimmage

Max protection – pass protection in which everyone stays in to block, except one or two wide receivers

Penalty – a foul that is committed on offense or defense

Plant leg – the leg that stays planted on the ground when the ball is kicked

Play – starts at either the snap from the center or at kickoff; most commonly occurs at the snap during a down

Playbook – a "plan of action" or strategy used to advance the ball

Pylon – orange markers in front and back of end zone to indicate touchdown or out of bounds

QB throwback pass – a trick play in which the running back fakes the run and throws it back to the quarterback

Quarterback – position that calls the plays on offense and receives the ball from center. He can hand it off, throw it, or run it.

Red zone – 20 yards to the goal line

Running back – a player who runs with the football on offense

Screen pass – pass play in which the running back appears to be blocking prior to slipping out for a pass with lineman blocking out in front

Slip screen – quick pass laterally to the wide receiver

Swing pass – pass route run by running back while sprinting towards the sideline

Touchdown – when a team scores 6 points by advancing the ball into the opponent's end zone

Trip – three wide receivers to one side of the offensive formation

"West Coast" offense – multiple formation offense that puts pressure on defensives laterally and vertically in the run and pass game

Wide receiver – player who catches passes from the quarterback

What are autoimmune diseases?

If it weren't for the immune system—the human body's natural defense against outside invaders—we would be sick all the time. This complex network of cells, organs, and molecules fights off things like bacteria and viruses 24 hours a day, from our head to our toes. It's a powerful protection when it's working for us, but can also be a powerful threat when it turns against us, in what's called an autoimmune disease ("auto" meaning self).

Autoimmune diseases in children are rare. When they occur they can be challenging to diagnose and difficult to treat. Doctors are still learning about this large group of mostly chronic illnesses—more than 80 in all—most of which have no cure yet. If your child has an autoimmune problem, much depends on figuring out what it is and then treating the condition aggressively.

Source: Boston Children's Hospital

Discussion Questions

1.) If you struck up a friendship with a new kid in town, and they confided in you that they are moving again because their father got a new job, what would you say to them?

2.) Turn to the person next to you and tell them about a time when you may have misjudged someone or judged someone harshly, only to find out that something else was going on with that person.

3.) How would you react if you were Buddy's teammate and Captain Cal came and apologized for stealing the ball and the playbook?

4.) Do you believe in superstitions, and if so, what superstitions do you have? How does a superstition affect your mindset?

5.) Captain Cal used his cell phone to steal photos of the Witches' playbook. Do you know anyone who has used cell phones inappropriately?

6.) When Beverly captain Cal took the ball, he said that Buddy's team won because of the football. Do you believe in magic? Do you believe the football was magical, or was the magic that Buddy and his team believed in themselves? If the football was actually magical, would you think it was unfair? What would you do if you found a magic football?

7.) When Buddy was injured during the ten-yard fight, he got up when he remembered his mom. Who in your life gives you the strength to keep getting back up, no matter what?

Acknowledgments

I lived through a challenging time to say the least when writing this book. This time allowed me to slow down, pause, and realize what truly is important in life. I thank God for continuing to place angelic brothers and sisters in my life.

It was a blessing to collaborate with Mascot Books' CEO Naren Aryal, who believed in my vision. Thank to my editor Megan Doyle for your attention to detail. Susan Roberts, your leadership and diligent work kept the project on track. My illustrator Chiara brought all the illustrations to life; you are a true artist, and seeing the final proofs brought moisture to my eyes.

My parents' input and support always allows me to keep an open mind. You are both my heroes and have never missed a moment. The same is true for my brothers Michael and Eric, who are some of my biggest supporters. Michael, "Coach Mike," you gave me a magical childhood. You allowed me to dream big and gave me the greatest gift a kid could ask for: unconditional love and support. You will always be a coach that I will reflect on for truly making me believe I could accomplish anything in sports, and that size does not matter. My older brother, Eric "Big E," you inspired me as a kid, and thanks for always being a sounding board.

To my mother-in-law Cathi for her input on the illustrations to help bring the magic out of them. To my late sister-in-law

Gena, you passed too soon and left a void in our hearts. Kaylee and Kelsey will carry your legacy.

Thanks to those who are working in research of Prosaic Arthritis, Lupus, and autoimmune diseases, and the staff at Boston Children's who have been working with Gianna.

My friends at Little Lambs and Iron Tree, thanks for your support. Please visit www.littlelambsintl.org to support their children.

Pasquale "Papa" Stellato, Nana, Nonno, thanks for paving the way. Cousin Nicole and Auntie Laure for always having my back.

The friendship of Dean Martino and Al DeFatta has been invaluable to me in several ways. For many years I have been able to turn to you both at any hour. To the late Lawrie Bertram, thanks for believing in me and being a molder of thousands of students. To my childhood friend Bulldog, we shared so many amazing memories as kids. Gus Martucci, thanks for your friendship and support. A-Train, you always had my back and my respect.

Thank you to my endorsers, who were very busy and took the time to read the manuscript and believe in the mission.

To my Pop Warner coaches, Coach Howie Olson, Coach Bruce Riccardi, and Coach Michael Stellato, thanks for believing in me. You all brought everlasting magical memories to my life. Coach "Cal" Caldera will live forever in my heart. The imprint on my heart is a brand I will always keep close.

To each of my childhood teammates, I will always hold close the bond we created. To every kid who dreams of doing something extraordinary through sport. It can happen with a relentless work ethic, passion, grit, and faith. Never settle, and never give up on your dream.

To Owa, whom I miss and will always be my source of inspiration.

My daughters, Gianna, Sophia-Bella, Giulietta, and Siena, are a constant source of strength. I learn from you every day. The four of you are so unique and introduced me to a world that I never knew existed. Gianna, you are a driving force behind my motivation to bring awareness to these challenging diseases you and so many face. Your courage is so inspiring. Sophia, your thoughtfulness, sincerity, and drive are so inspiring. You're the staple for the words, *work ethic*. Your great aunt Laurie is smiling down as you keep her passion for animals. Giulietta, you are so fun to be around. Your energy and sense of humor bring a smile to my face. I cherish our park visits, basketball, and time in the pool together. Siena Sicily, I missed so much time with your sisters chasing a dream and building a business. I cannot put onto paper how you make me feel. You're a blessing and an instant stress reliever. You help me understand the world more deeply. Family is what is really important. My late Boxer dog Sly is always in my heart.

I would particularly like to thank my wife, best friend, and love, Krista, for raising four amazing kids and many would argue five, which includes myself. You're my true other half and make me whole every day. You make every day magical; your unselfishness, honesty, and patience amaze me, and you're truly the keeper of my soul. Thanks for giving me direction and faith to put the pen to paper again.

About the Authors

Photo credit: Pete Tschudy

Sean Stellato
Author of *No Backing Down*
NFL Sports Agent

NFL sports agent Sean Stellato has never backed down from a challenge. Once told "skinny kids don't make it in sports full of giants," Sean defied the naysayers to become a star quarterback at Salem High School during a tumultuous time in the town's history. After high school, Stellato attended The Gunnery School, then carried the valuable lessons of perseverance and standing tall against adversity to his college football career at Marist College. He was named a Division 1 dual athlete and also excelled in the classroom. Post-college, Sean played several seasons in the Arena Football League and today serves as an NFL sports agent. He is the founder of Stellato Enhanced Sports.

Known for his dogged determination and unparalleled work ethic, Sean Stellato has negotiated multi-million dollar player contracts for a host of NFL stars, and endorsement deals with several big companies. Sean takes particular pride in his membership in the Salem High School Hall of Fame, Gunnery School Hall of Fame, and the National Italian-American Sports Hall of Fame (NE Chapter). As founder of the All-American Fundamental Showcase, he helps pave a smoother path for the next generation of athletes by providing a skills tutorial for high school athletes looking to demonstrate their talent to local and national institutions. Sean previously wrote about Salem High School in his book, *No Backing Down: The Story of the 1994 Salem High School Football Team.*

Stellato's Pop Warner photo.
The inspiration for Buddy.

Gianna Stellato is a student at the Boston Ballet School. She was recently diagnosed with auto-immune diseases, but she doesn't let that stop her from pursuing her passion of being a ballerina. Outside of dancing, she loves to read, write, and help spread awareness about her condition.

Photo credit: Michael Gray

Buddy, Sophia, Dad, and Sly as
drawn by Sophia Stellato

The message of "no backing down" is now becoming
a larger movement to promote strength and character
under the umbrella of No Backing Down. The mission
is to provide well-rounded educational programs in
environments that encourage individual growth, promote
personal character development, and prepare individuals
to meet the diverse challenges of their futures.